When The People Are Away

For Kievan best wishes
& well done on the
mural from
Linda Birch

For my Godson,
Lucas Gabriel

First published in the UK by Picture Lions 1992
Picture Lions is an imprint of the Children's Division,
part of HarperCollins Publishers Limited.
9 8 7 6 5 4 3 2

Text © Ann Jungman 1992
Illustrations © Linda Birch 1992

Printed and bound in Great Britain
by BPCC Paulton Books

This book is set in Goudy 18/22

When The People Are Away

ANN JUNGMAN ~ LINDA BIRCH

PictureLions

An Imprint of HarperCollins*Publishers*

The children stood in the drive and cried.

"What's wrong?" asked Mum. "Don't you want to go and visit Grannie?"

"Yes," sniffed the boys, "but what about the cats? Will they be all right without us?"

"Don't worry," said Mum. "I've arranged for Sandra from over the road to feed them. You'll be all right, won't you cats?"

The two ginger cats sat in the drive and blinked at Mum.

"Come on boys," she said, "we'll be back in a few days."

"Well," said Magnus, "that's got rid of them for a while."

"I shall miss them," said Lulu.

"Nonsense," replied Magnus, "you know what they say - when the cat's away the mice will play."

"But Magnus, we haven't gone away and there aren't any mice."

"Well I've adapted the saying a bit, Lulu. Now it's when the people are away the cats will play." Magnus told her. "We'll play something different each night. Tonight we're going to have an all-night disco. Go and spread the word."

So later that night all the cats in the neighbourhood trooped into Magnus and Lulu's house.

There was lots of loud music and the cats danced all night.

For the whole of the next day the cats slept. When
Sandra came to feed them they didn't even hear her.

When Magnus and Lulu woke up, Lulu asked, "What are
we going to do tonight?"
"Tonight," Magnus informed her, "we are going to have
an all-night video show. Go and spread the word."

So that night the cats gathered and watched cartoons.
"It's Tom and Jerry." Magnus told them. "You all know
what to do."
So the cats cheered every time Tom the cat came on
but booed when Jerry the mouse came on.
The cats really enjoyed themselves.

The next evening Lulu asked again,
"What are we going to do tonight Magnus?"
"An all-night all-in wrestling competition," Magnus
told her. "Go and spread the word."

That night all the cats turned up looking very tough.
Magnus made them form two lines.
"Everyone is to wrestle with the cat opposite them,"
he said. "The winners will fight each other."

So the cats had great fun wrestling with each other. In the end Magnus won. "Magnus is the champ," they cried.

The next day Lulu asked, "Can we have a night off, I'm very tired." "Certainly not," said Magnus, "the people will be back soon. Tonight is the Great Cat Singing Competition. Go on, go and spread the word."

That night the cats arrived looking very excited.

"You musn't sing too loudly." Magnus told them.
"People don't like the sound of cats singing, though
I don't know why."
"We'll be very quiet," promised the cats.
So the cats each sang in turn. They were very good.
But the best was Lulu. She sang and played the guitar.
It was a sad song and everyone cried.

The next day Magnus looked at the calendar.
"Our people are coming back," he told Lulu. "This is our last night."
"Can we have another singing competition?" asked Lulu hopefully.
"No," said Magnus. "Tonight we will have a grand midnight feast. Spread the word. Everyone is to bring something to eat and no tins. We're all tired of tins."

So one cat brought a carton of cream,

another brought
two kippers,

another brought some liver,

another brought some chicken and another brought some prawns.

"What a feast we are going to have," said Magnus.

That night the cats ate and ate until there was nothing left.

A big black cat stood up on the piano. "Friends, friends," he cried. "Pray silence for a toast. To Magnus and Lulu, our hosts and friends. May their people go away very often." "To Magnus and Lulu and their people," chorused all the cats. "Thanks," said Magnus.
"Speech, speech," cried the cats.
Magnus climbed up on to the piano.
"Friends," he said. "Fellow cats. We've all had lots of fun. Now, as you know, our people are coming back. Please help us with the clearing up, so that no one knows what has been happening. That way we can do it again."

So, very soon, two of the cats were loading the dishwasher,

another three pushed the hoover around with difficulty,
two others tidied up, someone dusted and another
polished the silver.

By morning no one could have known that the cats had had:

A disco,

an all-in wrestling competition,

an all-night video session,

a singing competition

and a midnight feast.

As soon as the children got back they rushed into the house to find Magnus and Lulu. "Did you miss us a lot?" they asked giving them both a cuddle.
But Magnus and Lulu just stretched and yawned and then curled up in their basket and went back to sleep.

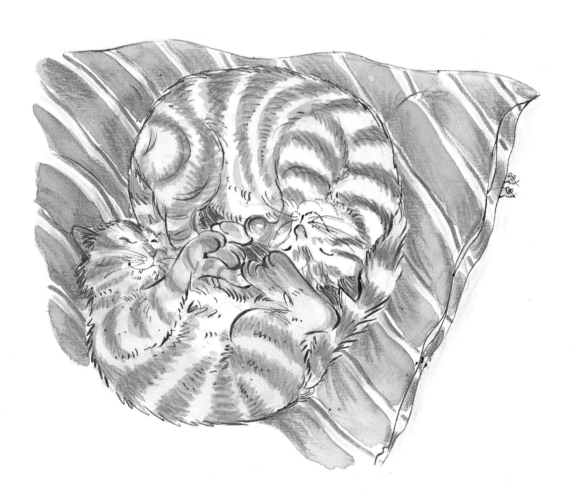